Lazy Cat Crazy Cat belongs to:

For Mum and Dad
- Mel

For Laurelou
- Delphine

Published in Ireland by O'Donnell Press,
12 Coolemoyne Park, Jordanstown, Co. Antrim BT37 0RP
Tele[illegible]93
Email address: b.odonnell93@ntlworld.com
www.[illegible]om

A CIP catalogue record of this book is available from the British Library.

Printed in Ireland by GPS Colour Graphics Ltd.

ISBN 0-9553325-0-8

1 2 3 4 5 6 7 8 9 10

O'DONNELL PRESS

Lazy Cat Crazy Cat

The tale of a Dublin cat

Mel Fisher
Delphine Thomas

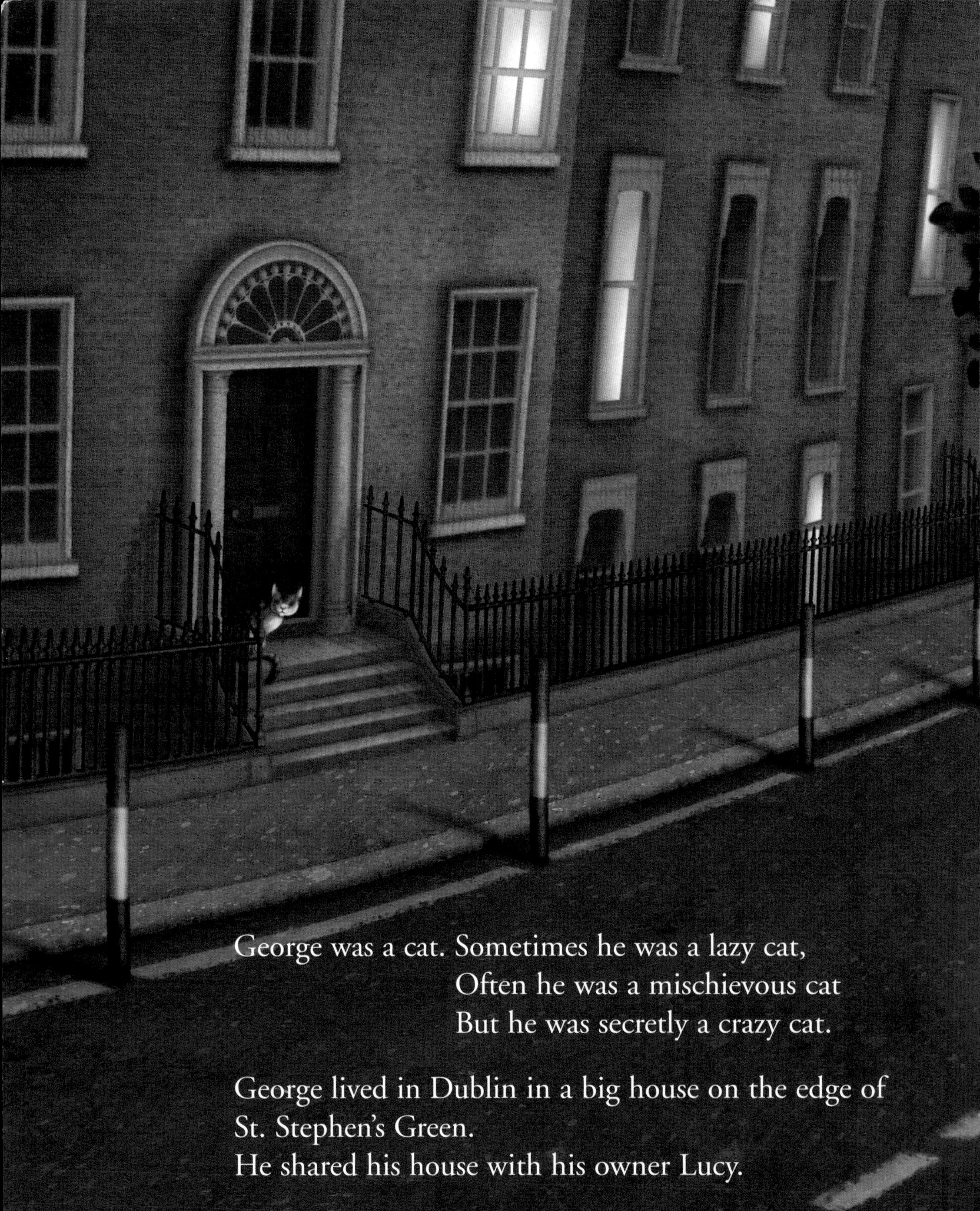

George was a cat. Sometimes he was a lazy cat,
Often he was a mischievous cat
But he was secretly a crazy cat.

George lived in Dublin in a big house on the edge of St. Stephen's Green.
He shared his house with his owner Lucy.

During the day he loved to curl up on Lucy's knee, purring contentedly as she stroked his head and scratched his ears. When he was hungry he s l o w l y s t r e t c h e d and before you could say 'lazy cat' he disappeared off Lucy's knee. With a cheeky grin he crept over to the fire and licked every last drop of cream from the saucer.

Yes, George enjoyed his lazy days!

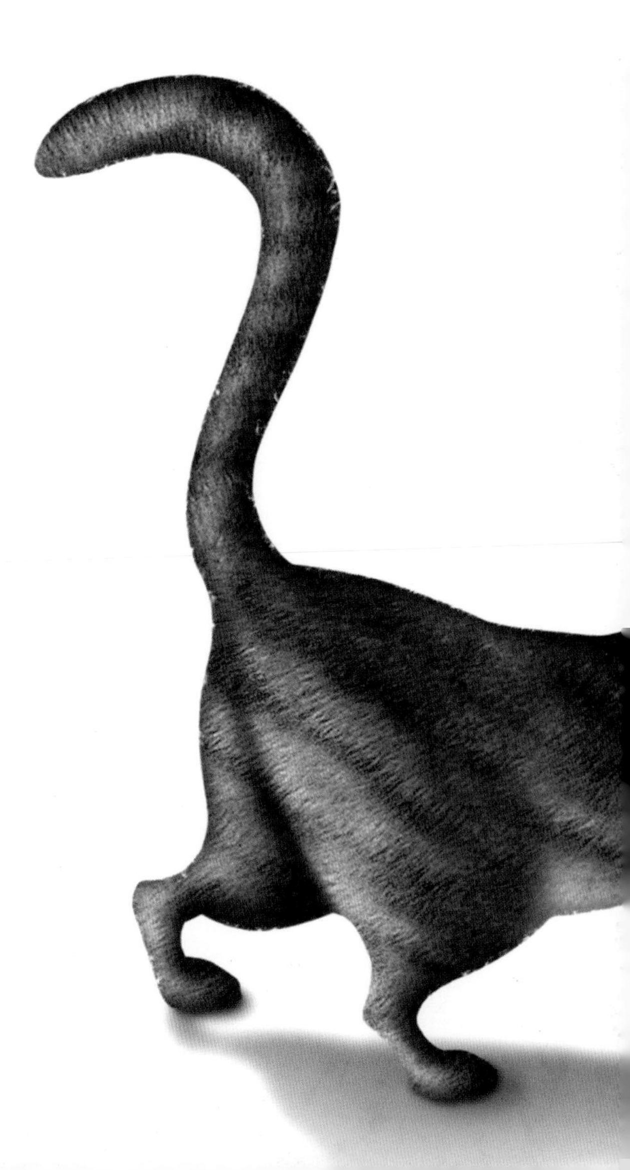

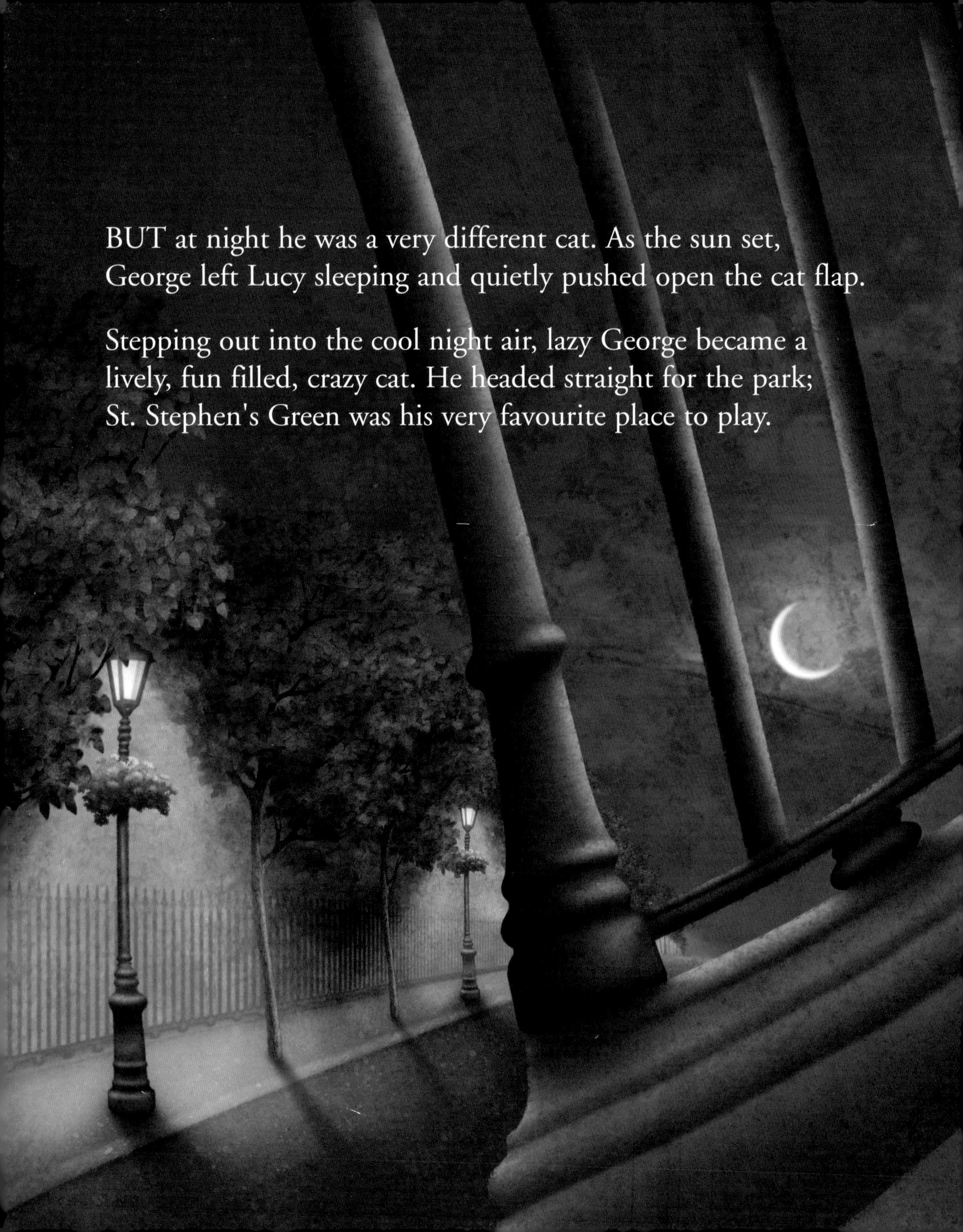

BUT at night he was a very different cat. As the sun set, George left Lucy sleeping and quietly pushed open the cat flap.

Stepping out into the cool night air, lazy George became a lively, fun filled, crazy cat. He headed straight for the park; St. Stephen's Green was his very favourite place to play.

Here you would never guess you were in the heart of a big city. Acres of grass and trees and flowers hid the grey buildings and the only people present at night were the tall, menacing statues, which George knew would never move. He felt safe, no cars, no people, just cats (and other animals)! The park keeper closed the gates at dusk and only those small enough to fit through the railings could enter. Moonlight danced on the paths and lit the park just enough for animals to play.

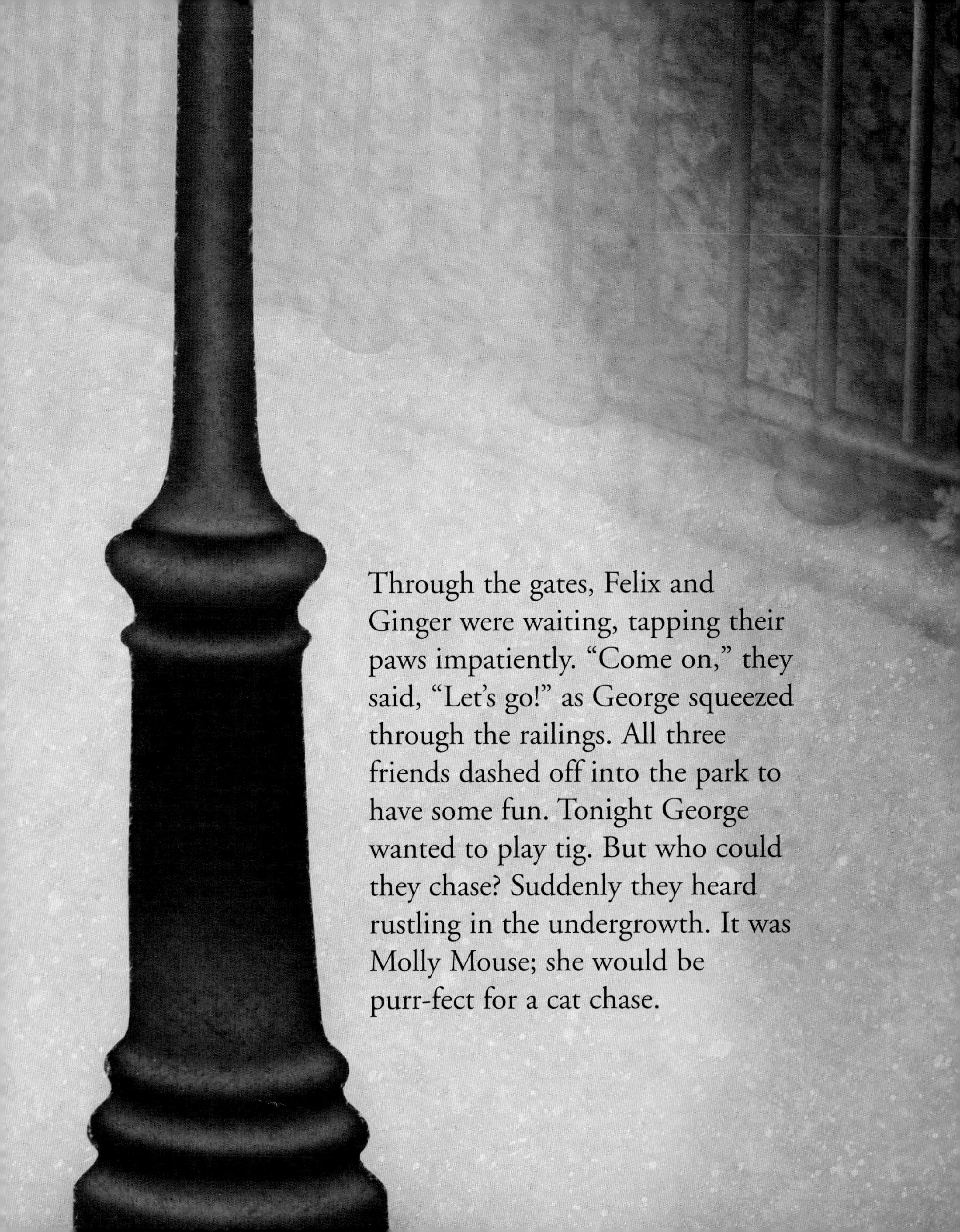

Through the gates, Felix and Ginger were waiting, tapping their paws impatiently. “Come on,” they said, “Let’s go!” as George squeezed through the railings. All three friends dashed off into the park to have some fun. Tonight George wanted to play tig. But who could they chase? Suddenly they heard rustling in the undergrowth. It was Molly Mouse; she would be purr-fect for a cat chase.

They chased her along the river path until she darted into a small gap in the rockery. She chuckled with glee from the safety of her tiny cave, “You can’t catch me!”

But George’s paw slipped easily through the opening and he poked her with his claws.

“Ouch!” yelled Molly as she darted out and fled to the flower bed with Felix, Ginger and George hot on her heels!

She scampered up the trunk of a towering willow tree, whose branches arched over the river. Like a tightrope walker she carefully tiptoed out along a slender branch. Those mischievous cats couldn't reach her here. But crazy George followed her along the branch. The whole branch began to wobble with the weight, then it started to shake and shake and SHAKE.

Molly held on tight, with her eyes firmly shut.
George began to bounce as if he were on a trampoline and to everyone's horror he was catapulted high into the air. George flew so far above the ground, he saw right over Dublin city. "Wow! What a view," he thought as he saw millions of tiny lights trace the outline of the city streets. This was fun but THEN he stopped soaring up and began to fall down.

Oh no, this wasn't so much fun after all! Faster and faster he fell until SPLASH, George landed in the river. He made such a huge splash, he soaked and woke some poor ducks who were happily sleeping with their heads tucked under their wings. Not sure what was going on, they quacked angrily at George and flapped their wings to let him know he was NOT welcome.

It wasn't long before Felix, Ginger and Molly burst out laughing, as they watched George splutter and splash in the water, trying to escape the angry ducks. They laughed and laughed until tears ran down their cheeks.

George, with water dripping off his fur, leapt out of the shallow river. With a twinkle in his eye, he shook himself so hard he soaked his amused friends. George was now dry and everyone else was WET! George raced after Molly, watched closely by Felix and Ginger. He darted in and out of the flower beds, round and round the fountains until he collapsed exhausted in the mossy grass laughing with sheer delight.
Yes tonight had been lots of fun!

Felix and Ginger once again joined George and together they lay gazing at the dark sky, sighing contentedly as they watched the morning sun peek out from the horizon. They knew this night's adventure was over and it was time to leave the Green. Reluctantly, they all trudged to the gate, bid farewell until the next night, and hurried off home.

George pushed his way back in through the cat flap. Lucy found him as usual, when she came downstairs for breakfast, curled up fast asleep in the armchair.
"There's my lazy cat!" said Lucy gently stroking his fur.
"If only she knew! Lazy at dawn AND crazy at dusk," whispered George with a mischievous wink....

but shhh that's our secret!

Enjoy more great picture books from O'Donnell Press

ISBN 0-9553325-1-6

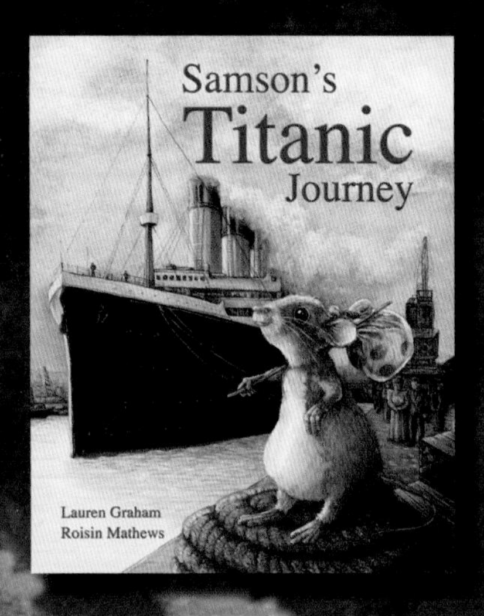

ISBN 0-9546163-5-9

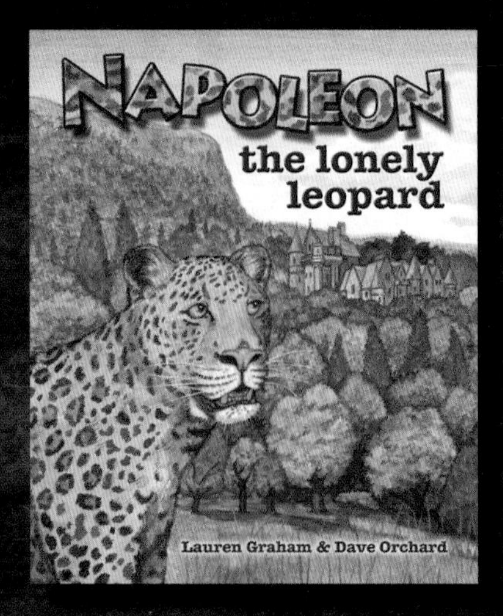

ISBN 0-9546163-7-5

ISBN 0-9546163-6-7

ISBN 0-9546163-1-6

www.odonnellpress.com